MR. CLEVER

by Roger Hargreaves

KU-111-675

Mr Clever was quite the cleverest person ever.

The Cleverest Person In The World!

And, he knew it!

"Oh, I am so very very CLEVER," he used to say.

To himself more often than not.

He lived in Cleverland where, as you may know, everybody and everything is us clever as can be.

In Cleverland clever trees manage to grow apples and oranges at the same time!

In Cleverland clever flowers get up and go for a walk!

Clever worms drive around in cars all day!

And clever elephants play tennis!

Oh yes, Cleverland is quite the most clever place.

Would you like to live there?

Mr Clever does.

"Oh, I am so very very CLEVER to build such a clever house," he used to go around telling everybody.

One morning, Mr Clever was awakened by his special Mr Clever alarm clock.

Not only did it wake you up by ringing a bell: it also switched on a light; and said "Good morning"; and made a cup of tea; and showed what the weather was going to be; and told you the time; and showed you the date. It also whistled cheerfully while it was doing all that!

Mr Clever yawned, got up, washed, cleaned his teeth (with his special Mr Clever toothbrush which squeezed toothpaste on to the brush out of the handle), and went downstairs for breakfast.

He popped a slice of bread into his special Mr Clever electric toaster.

Which not only toasted the bread, but also spread it with butter and marmalade, AND cut off the crusts!

After breakfast he went for a long walk.

An extremely long walk.

In fact, such a long walk that he walked all the way out of Cleverland, although he didn't know it.

He met somebody who was also out for a walk.

Do you know who it was?

That's right.

Mr Happy!

"Hello," cried Mr Clever. "I'm The Cleverest Person In The World!"

"Oh good," said Mr Happy. "Then you must be clever enough to make up a really good joke to tell me."

He laughed.

"Jokes make me happy," he explained.

Mr Clever's face fell.

"I don't know any jokes," he admitted.

"Well, that's not very clever of you, is it?" said Mr Happy, and went off.

Mr Clever went on.

And do you know who he met next?

That's right.

Mr Greedy!

"Hello," cried Mr Clever. "I'm The Cleverest Person In The World!"

"Oh good," said Mr Greedy. "Then you can tell me the recipe of the world's most delicious dish."

He licked his lips.

"I like food," he explained.

Mr Clever's face fell.

"I can't cook," he admitted. "And I don't know any recipes!"

"Well, that's not very clever of you, is it?" said Mr Greedy, and went off.

In search of food.

Mr Clever went on.

And who do you think he met next?

Yes.

Mr Forgetful!

"Hello," cried Mr Clever. "I'm The Cleverest Person In The World!"

"Oh good," said Mr Forgetful. "Then you can tell me what my name is."

He smiled apologetically.

"I've forgotten," he explained.

Mr Clever's face fell for the third time that morning.

"But I don't know your name," he admitted. "We've only just met!"

"Well, that's not very clever of you, is it?" said Mr Forgetful, and he too went off.

Forgetting to say goodbye!

And so it went on. All day.

Mr Clever couldn't tell Mr Sneeze the cure for a cold.

And he couldn't tell Mr Small how he could grow bigger.

And he couldn't tell Mr Jelly what the secret of being brave was.

And he couldn't tell Mr Topsy-Turvy how to talk the round way right.

I mean the right way round.

A not very clever day!

Not at all.

Not a bit.

As by now he wasn't feeling anything like The Cleverest Person In The World, Mr Clever decided he'd better go home.

He passed a pair of worms who were having a chat.

"Who's that?" asked one worm.

"That," replied the other worm, "is Mr Clever, The Cleverest Person In The World, on his way home to Cleverland!"

The first worm thought.

"He can't be that clever," he replied . . .

. . . "he's going the wrong way!"

Fantastic offers for Mr. Men fans!

Collect all your Mr. Men or Little Miss books in these superb durable collectors' cases!
Only £5.99 inc. postage and packing, these wipe-clean, hard-wearing cases will give all your Mr. Men or Little Miss books a beautiful new home!

Keep track of your collection with this giant-sized double-sided Mr. Men and Little Miss Collectors' poster.
Collect 6 tokens and we will send you a brilliant giant-sized double-sided collectors' poster! Simply tape a £1 coin to cover postage and packaging in the space provided and fill out the form overleaf.

STICK £1 COIN HERE (for poster only)

cut along the dotted line and return this whole page

Only need a few Mr. Men or Little Miss to complete your set? You can order any of the titles on the back of the books from our Mr. Men order line on 0870 787 1724. Orders should be delivered between 5 and 7 working days.

--- **TO BE COMPLETED BY AN ADULT** ---

To apply for any of these great offers, ask an adult to complete the details below and send this whole page with the appropriate payment and tokens, to: MR. MEN CLASSIC OFFER, PO BOX 715, HORSHAM RH12 5WG

☐ Please send me a giant-sized double-sided collectors' poster.
AND ☐ I enclose 6 tokens and have taped a £1 coin to the other side of this page.

☐ Please send me ☐ Mr. Men Library case(s) and/or ☐ Little Miss library case(s) at £5.99 each inc P&P

☐ I enclose a cheque/postal order payable to Egmont UK Limited for £.................

OR ☐ Please debit my MasterCard / Visa / Maestro / Delta account (delete as appropriate) for £.................

Card no. ☐☐☐☐ ☐☐☐☐ ☐☐☐☐ ☐☐☐☐ ☐☐☐☐   Security code ☐☐☐

Issue no. (if available) ☐   Start Date ☐☐/☐☐/☐☐   Expiry Date ☐☐/☐☐/☐☐

Fan's name: ....   Date of birth: ....

Address: ....

....

....   Postcode: ....

Name of parent / guardian: ....

Email for parent / guardian: ....

Signature of parent / guardian: ....

Please allow 28 days for delivery. Offer is only available while stocks last. We reserve the right to change the terms of this offer at any time and we offer a 14 day money back guarantee. This does not affect your statutory rights. Offers apply to UK only.

☐ We may occasionally wish to send you information about other Egmont children's books.
If you would rather we didn't, please tick this box.

Ref: MRM 001

cut along the dotted line and return this whole page